STEP INTO READING®

3

STEP

READING ON YOUR OWN

P9-CEO-058

Frederick

by Leo Lionni

Random House 🏠 New York

All along the meadow
where the cows grazed
and the horses ran,
there was an old stone wall.

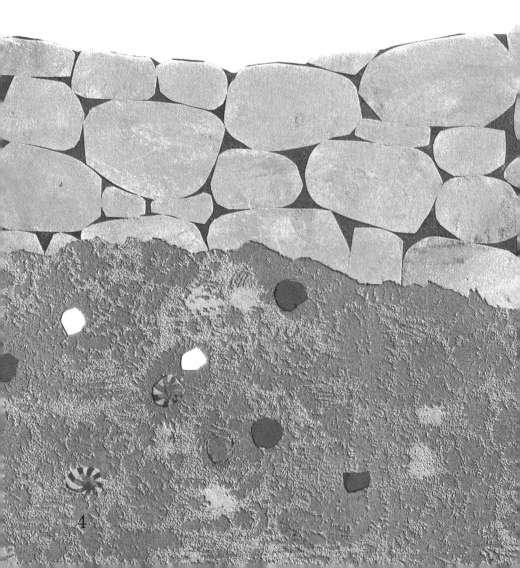

5

In that wall, not far
from the barn and the granary,
a chatty family of field mice
had their home.

7

But the farmers had
moved away,
the barn was abandoned,
and the granary stood empty.
And since winter
was not far off, the little mice
began to gather corn and nuts
and wheat and straw.
They all worked day and night.
All—except Frederick.

"Frederick, why don't you
   work?" they asked.
"I *do* work," said Frederick.
"I gather sun rays
   for the cold dark winter days."

And when they saw Frederick
sitting there,
staring at the meadow,
they said, "And now, Frederick?"

"I gather colors,"

answered Frederick simply.

"For winter is gray."

And once

Frederick seemed half asleep.

"Are you dreaming, Frederick?"

they asked reproachfully.

But Frederick said,

"Oh no, I am gathering words.

"For the winter days
are long and many,
and we'll run out
of things to say."

The winter days came,
and when the first snow fell
the five little field mice
took to their hideout
in the stones.

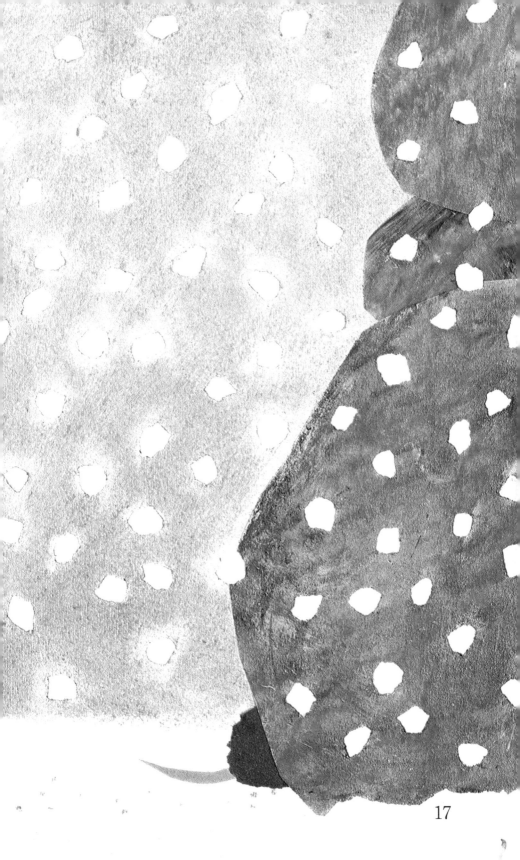

In the beginning
there was lots to eat,
and the mice told stories
of foolish foxes and silly cats.
They were a happy family.

19

But little by little
they had nibbled up
most of the nuts and berries,
the straw was gone,
and the corn was only
a memory.

It was cold in the wall
and no one felt like chatting.

Then they remembered
what Frederick had said
about sun rays and
colors and words.

"What about *your* supplies,
Frederick?" they asked.

"Close your eyes,"
   said Frederick,
   as he climbed on a big stone.
"Now I send you
   the rays of the sun.
   Do you feel how their
   golden glow . . ."

And as Frederick spoke
of the sun
the four little mice
began to feel warmer.
Was it Frederick's voice?
Was it magic?

"And how about the colors,
  Frederick?"
  they asked anxiously.
"Close your eyes again,"
  Frederick said.
  And when he told them
  of the blue periwinkles,
  the red poppies
  in the yellow wheat,

and the green leaves of the
berry bush, they saw the colors
as clearly as if they had been
painted in their minds.

"And the words, Frederick?"
Frederick cleared his throat,
waited a moment, and then,
as if from a stage, he said:

"Who scatters snowflakes?
Who melts the ice?
Who spoils the weather?
Who makes it nice?
Who grows the
four-leaf clovers in June?
Who dims the daylight?
Who lights the moon?
Four little field mice who live
in the sky. Four little
field mice . . . like you and I.

"One is the Springmouse
who turns on the showers.
Then comes the Summer
who paints in the flowers.
The Fallmouse is next
with walnuts and wheat.
And Winter is last . . .
with little cold feet. Aren't we
lucky the seasons are four?
Think of a year with one less . . .
or one more!"

When Frederick had finished,
they all applauded.
"But Frederick," they said,
"you are a poet!"
Frederick blushed, took a bow,
and said shyly, "I know it."

LEO LIONNI wrote and illustrated more than forty picture books in his lifetime, including four Caldecott Honor Books—*Inch by Inch, Swimmy, Frederick,* and *Alexander and the Wind-Up Mouse.* He died in 1999 at the age of 89.

Praise for Leo Lionni

"If the picture book is a new visual art form in our time, Leo Lionni is certain to be judged a master of the genre."

—Selma Lanes, *The New York Times*

Guess the Word

How well do you know *Frederick*?
Can you remember the story
by reading the sentences below?

This story is about a  named
Frederick.

Frederick and the other mice are getting
ready for  .

The mice gather so they
will be prepared.

But Frederick gathers words.
When it snows, the mice hide in a

 .

In the winter, Frederick helps the mice feel
warm and see .

The poem in this story is about the
four seasons.

Seasons

In this story, the mice get ready
for winter. Do you know
all four seasons? Which season
matches each picture?

spring   summer

fall   winter

What doesn't belong?

Do you remember the pictures from
the story? Which one is different
from the rest?

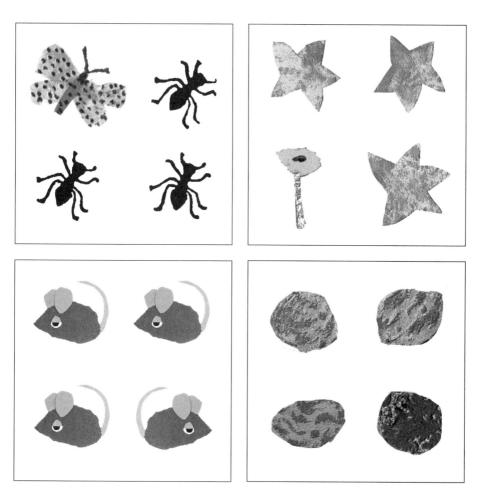

Alexander is a real mouse, but everyone loves Willy, the wind-up mouse. Can Alexander become a wind-up mouse, too?

STEP INTO READING

Alexander and the Wind-Up Mouse

by Leo Lionni